DARK HALLOWEEN KNIGHT

A KNIGHT'S RIDGE EMPIRE SHORT STORY

TRACY LORRAINE

TRACY LORRAINE

NOTE

Chronologically, *Dark Halloween Knight* falls at the end of *Wicked Princess*, the second book in my new *Knight's Ridge Empire* series but there is no reason why you can't read it before, there are no spoilers!

BLURB

I've lived my entire life in the shadows...

Sheltered yet painfully aware of the haunting reality of who my family really is.

I'm tired of being the good girl— of doing everything I'm told. Halloween seems like the perfect time to explore my hidden desires.

And that's exactly how I end up in the arms of a masked mystery guy.

He doesn't handle me like glass. He takes exactly what he wants and gives me everything

I didn't know I needed— until he vanishes into the darkness leaving me with one burning question...

Who was my mysterious knight that introduced me to the dark side?

CHAPTER ONE

The Knight's Ridge Halloween parties are legendary.

Or at least that's what I've told my two new best friends, who've only recently started at school.

The truth is, I've never been to one.

Even last year, Nico, my overbearing, arrogant asshole of a brother, wouldn't let me go.

I'd bought a costume and everything.

I should have just gone. He'd have been none the wiser as he partied with his idiot friends and flirted with every girl who so much as looked his way.

But even if the prospect of that wasn't

unappealing enough. I knew that it wasn't just Nico who wouldn't want me there.

I didn't fit in.

I never have.

Everyone is either too scared to come anywhere near me for fear of what Nico and the guys will do to them, or they just use me to get to them.

So my costume never saw the light of day and I spent the night opening our front door and handing out sweets to any kids who were brave enough to come to our door.

There weren't many of them. Most are part of the Family.

But now, I'm done with being nothing more than a pawn in other students' games to get close to the big bad mafia boys of Knight's Ridge College. I'm more than just a ladder others can climb to improve their social standing.

I'm Callista Cirillo.

Mafia princess.

Long-suffering little sister and daughter of powerful men.

Well, tonight that ends.

Tonight, I'm shedding that skin and

dragging on another that looks more like my two new best friends.

And right on cue, the doorbell rings.

I'm home alone, aside from the grumpy fuck in the basement. But there's no way he'll poke his head up to answer, so I make my way through the house with excitement quickly filling my veins for what the rest of the night might hold.

Pulling the front door open, I find Emmie with her usual scowl on her beautiful face.

"Glad to see you're excited about tonight," I quip, allowing her inside.

It's not the first time she's been here, but she still looks around somewhat in awe. I get it, our house is pretty insane. Since Stella's... accident a few weeks ago, we've been hanging out more and more. She's yet to invite me back to her place though. She's not said why, but I'm pretty sure it's probably got something to do with the fact her dad is banging Miss Hill, our Student Welfare Director at Knight's Ridge.

She might be my opposite in every way, but also, she's everything I've ever wanted in a friend. And someone I just know that my parents will hate, if they're even in our house long enough to run into her.

She's completely unconcerned by what my last name is, how big our house is, or any of the bullshit that surrounds my life.

She's just... herself. Unapologetic, slightly rude, gorgeous, and a total bad influence. I love her, Stella too.

They both stumbled into my life when I needed them the most and I couldn't be more grateful.

I've done things in the past few weeks I never would have if it weren't for them. I got wasted, crashed one of my brother's parties, shot a freaking gun, smoked a joint. Hell, I've even got a fake ID in my purse and have been inside an actual nightclub... underage.

I know it's probably not all that wild in most people's books, but when you consider the girl I was before the start of this school year, then it's insane.

And I love it.

Emmie laughs to herself as she follows me up to my room as she takes in all our family photographs on the stairs.

I know what's amusing her, it has done so every time she's been here.

Emmie might have an interesting family as well, seeing as her grandfather is the prez of the Royal Reapers MC—a secret both Stella and I have been sworn to keep—but it doesn't stop her disbelief every time she sees that photo of the boys in their suits.

"Fucking mafia," she mutters in amusement.

"Come on, Princess. It's time to party."

"Don't call me that," she snaps. "Don't ever fucking call me that."

Spinning around, I hold my bedroom door open for her to enter, running my eyes down her outfit.

She's right, she looks nothing like a princess in her customised band tee, ripped black denim skirt, fishnets, and biker boots.

She looks hot, and completely out of place in my sugary pink princess bedroom.

"I got drinks. Pizza will be here in a bit."

"Sweet." She toes off her boots and launches herself at the bed after grabbing a bottle of pink premixed cocktails that I bought specially for the occasion.

She twists the top off and takes a sip.

"Jesus," she mutters, lifting the bottle to look at the label. "Was this the best you could come up with?"

Laughing at her reaction, I refrain from telling her that I've hidden the good stuff and send a message to Stella asking her to hurry the hell up.

I stare at the screen to see if she's going to reply, or even read it.

"She's probably too busy bouncing on Seb's dick to reply," Emmie mutters, correctly guessing who I'm messaging.

I smother a laugh and put my phone down on the dresser.

"That much sex can't be healthy."

"Says the virgin."

"That's rich. How many guys have you been anywhere near since starting at Knight's Ridge?"

"Not anywhere near enough, that's for damn sure," she complains, lifting the pink glittery drink to her lips once more.

"Well, tonight is the night, Princess Ramsey." She gives me a death glare over her bottle, and I can't help but laugh.

The doorbell cuts through the house once more. "Pizza! I'll be right back. Don't go anywhere, and do not go looking for the costumes. You gotta wait for Stella."

She rolls her eyes at me, putting on a bored face, but it's all an act. I know she's secretly excited for what tonight might hold, deep, deep down. I just hope that all my words about how awesome this party is going to be don't fall flat and make me look like a complete moron.

Racing down the stairs, I grab the pizza boxes from the delivery guy, the scent of the tomato sauce and cheese making my stomach growl loudly, before the sound of voices from the back of the house filter down to me and thankfully drown it out.

"Ah, look what the cat dragged in," I say, wrapping my hand around Stella's upper arm and all but dragging her out of her boyfriend's hold.

"Hey," he complains, pulling her back. "I wasn't done."

"Piss off, Papatonis," I hiss, feeling brave. "You've had her all day. She's mine now."

His brows rise at the fact that I've talked

back to him when in the past I only would have cowered.

Yeah, take that, arsehole.

My chest puffs out in pride. Stella just laughs. Wrapping her arm around my shoulder she drops a quick kiss to Seb's lips and steps out of his hold.

"See you later, boyfriend."

Leading her away from her possessive arsehole, we head for the stairs, leaving him to go and find my brother in his den of sin, also known as our basement.

"Come on, Em's waiting. I told her she can't see the costumes until you're here."

Together we walk up the stairs, heading for our sassy friend.

"Finally, we didn't think he was going to let you out of his sight," Emmie says the second we join her, still exactly where she was laying on my bed. The bottle of her pink drink in her hand is almost empty.

She shoots me a knowing look because from the state of Stella's sex hair, it's not hard to guess that we were both right about what made her and Seb quite so late.

"I can't believe you got me in this thing. I don't wear pink. Ever," Emmie sasses, standing in front of the mirror two minutes before we need to leave.

I stand in the doorway to my bathroom with my matching pick jacket, but I've teamed mine with a swishy sixties skirt with an appliquéd dog on it. A wide smile is plastered on my lips as I watch my two girls put the finishing touches to their makeup and drain the bottle of vodka Emmie had stashed in her bag. She didn't even give me a chance to find my own stash.

She might act all bad-arse and sassy, but there's a heart of gold inside that girl. She could have pulled that out the second she got here and refused the silly pink drinks I bought—that they now know match our outfits to a T—but she didn't. She's also wearing my customised version of our pink ladies' jackets.

"Oh shut it," Stella snaps. "You look hot. And your ass in those leggings is insane. The guys won't be able to keep their hands off you."

"If you're talking about the guys downstairs

then they'd better well keep their fucking hands to themselves. I wouldn't fuck them with yours."

I smother a laugh. "I'm not sure any of them are brave enough. They might try to look scary and shit but they're a bunch of pussies," I tell them, taking a wobbly step forward. Damn, that pink drink might have been pretty, but it was stronger than I was expecting.

"Don't let them hear you say that," Stella mutters.

"I'm not interested in them."

"Such a shame because Th—" Emmie claps her hand over Stella's mouth, cutting off whatever she was going to say.

"Read my lips, Doukas. Theo fucking Cirillo is getting nowhere near me. He's a prick, and I can assure you, he has no interest in me in any way other than to be a pain in my fucking arse."

"Pain's good though, Em."

"Jesus. Shall we go?" Emmie says, turning to me, begging to be rescued.

"Yes! I'm so excited," I squeal, butterflies exploding in my belly.

It's obvious that the guys are already

waiting for us the second we open the door because their deep rumbling voices float up to us.

I glance at the girls on either side of me, take in their skintight leggings—they point blank refused the skirt option, can't say I was surprised—their tiny cropped tops, and pink jackets.

Yeah, the guys are going to lose their shit.

The second they appear in my vision at the bottom of the stairs, my breath catches in my throat. I am most definitely not attracted to them but holy hell they look insane right now.

"Whoa," Stella breathes while Emmie gasps, "holy shit."

Holy shit indeed. They're wearing matching vampire costumes, although each boy has styled it their own way. My dick of a brother has forgone a shirt entirely beneath his cape, probably hoping to attract the women with his abs. Seb's just wearing a tank, Theo has an almost completely unbuttoned shirt while Alex and Toby are wearing red waistcoats. But what really captures my attention are their eyes. They're all wearing freaky as fuck contact lenses.

Although, I must admit that seeing their faces all crinkle with laughter as they take in our outfits takes the terrifying edge off somewhat.

"What the fuck are you wearing?" Alex barks as Stella gets swept up once again by Seb.

"What? They're cute."

"Yeah, you could say that."

"Look," I say, spinning around to show them all my back, which makes them all laugh again, well everyone aside from Nico who is just like a miserable fuck.

"Don't tell me Emmie has—" Emmie spins, making them all smother laughs.

"Princess Emmie. Sorry, but I just can't see it," Toby says with amusement.

"She's no fucking princess," Theo scoffs, turning toward the front door and disappearing through it.

"What's his problem?"

The guys all share a knowing look. Something I used to be insanely jealous of when I barely had a real friend, let alone one I had that kind of connection with.

"He's a prick. I already told you that,"

Emmie says as if it's the most obvious thing in the world.

"Shall we?" Toby asks, being a total gentleman and holding his arm out for me.

"Let's," I say with a smile while Emmie mutters, "I need more vodka."

Toby chuckles beside me as we follow the others out.

He leads me to the car that Seb and Stella don't walk toward, and I can't help but smile.

"Don't wanna watch them dry hump in the car, huh?" I ask, desperately trying not to laugh. I shouldn't, I've recently had first-hand experience just how horrendous it is to walk in on a sibling doing something no other sibling should see. I totally get it, but I still can't help teasing him. I blame the vodka.

"Dry hump? Didn't you hear what they did to Alex on Friday night?"

It's a rhetorical question, I was there, well not in the car, but I witnessed the fall out of Alex's painful car journey with them screwing in the back.

"Lost your shirt, bro?" I ask, climbing into the car and finding Nico and his usual scowl. "What?" I ask when he doesn't respond with anything more than a grunt. "Still pissed your little sister grew a backbone?"

He stills a beat before his creepy fucking eyes turn on me.

"Do not get in any fucking trouble tonight, *kid*. And don't kiss any fucking Italians." His eyes narrow on me.

"Ah, that's right. I've got to ID any guy before I get close in case we're about to go to war with them."

My sarcasm doesn't improve Nico's mood at all.

"Stay the fuck away from anyone and you might just make it the entire night."

"You're full of shit. You'll lose yourself in the first willing pussy and forget I even exist."

His lips part in shock.

I get it. I've never stood up to him. Ever. But my bad influences are rubbing off on me. And, I'm discovering just how much fun it is to wind him up.

"Fucking pain in the arse," he mutters, running his fingers through his hair and messing up the slicked-back look he had going on.

Toby chuckles beside me as Emmie falls into the passenger seat.

"Let's get this show on the road," she announces, shooting our zombie driver a dangerous look.

Oh yeah, she's on a mission tonight. Just like I am.

My phone buzzes in my bag but I stop myself from reaching for it. It would be a really fucking bad idea while I'm sitting pinned between Nico and Toby.

I might be all for rebelling a little, but I haven't got a freaking death wish.

CHAPTER TWO

"Oh my God," I breathe as I walk into the old, abandoned building.

If it wasn't obvious on the drive toward it, then it really is now that all of my promises about an epic Halloween night were nothing but the truth. Thank fuck the rumours I'd heard from previous years weren't total bullshit.

"Okay," Emmie says, looping her arm through mine. "I am impressed. This place is insane."

"Right?" I look around at the smoke-filled entrance taking in the low hanging cobwebs, ghosts, zombies—which almost look too good not to be real—and everyone's costumes.

"Thank you," I shout over the pounding music when a zombie—one of Dad and uncle Damien's security guys—waves a tray of red drinks in front of us.

The floating eyeball gives me pause but I quickly recover and take the glass.

Emmie immediately knocks hers back, and I rush to do the same, the taste of sour cherry exploding in my mouth.

"Let's go explore." Emmie grabs my hand and pulls me farther into the abandoned building, leaving the others behind.

It used to be a pub apparently but was bought out to become luxury flats, but then that never happened and now it's just this dilapidated building that couldn't be more perfect for a night like this.

It's half demolished, walls have been pulled down ensuring that there's enough space for everyone, the windows are mostly smashed and doors half falling from their hinges. It's freaky as fuck, and I already know that it's not somewhere I'd ever want to be alone.

"ARGH," a blood-curdling scream rips from my lips when what I thought was a mannequin in the dark corner of the room not only moves but reaches out and touches me. "Fuck. Fuck," I bark, my heart racing so damn hard I'm surprised it doesn't pound straight out of my chest.

"Oh my God, that was classic," Emmie laughs beside me.

When I glance over, I find her bent over laughing with tears in her eyes.

"Alright, don't piss yourself," I mutter, irritated with myself that I'm clearly a total pussy.

"I think you're the only one out of the two of us that might have let a little pee out, Cal."

"I need another drink," I announce taking off across the room.

I spot a few people that I recognise from school. Teagan, our head bitch and her puppies are taking up one corner of the room each clearly trying to outdo each other with who could look more like a whore.

Teagan—swimsuit Barbie—notices me watching them and shoots me a death glare. It doesn't matter that I might be an invaluable member of her gym team, she can barely stand to look at me most days. Her two sidekicks—nurse Barbie and French maid Barbie—both turn their glares on me as well.

All I do in response is smile in their direction which makes their lips curl in even more disgust as they look me up and down before moving to Emmie beside me.

She growls, her entire body tensing, probably gearing up for another bitch fight with Teagan.

"Come on. Leave those whores to it. They're not worth it," I say, dragging her away before she starts something.

We're almost out of the room when someone—I've no idea who—catches my eye across the room. He's head to toe in black, a Batman mask covering his face and cape hanging from his neck. Even if I did know him, I've no way of trying to figure it out with only his jawline on show. But even still, something about the way he's looking at me makes my steps falter and my body temperature to spike.

"Who's that?" Emmie asks, noticing who's made me slow down.

"I've no idea."

"Well, he clearly wants you. You want me

to go over and make sure he's not got any Italian blood running through his body?" She takes off as if she's actually going to go and talk to him and I panic.

My fingers dig into her forearm a little too harshly as I drag her back.

"Don't even think about it," I hiss. "Come on, I need to pee and get a drink."

We find the toilets and slip past the female security zombie loitering at the door before we walk into a cubicle each.

Gathering up my skirt, I sit down but quickly pull my phone out.

Ant: Have a great night. Gutted I can't be there. ;)

The little winky face only increases the butterflies that took flight in my belly from just seeing his name.

With a smile, I tap out a reply.

I know I shouldn't still be talking to him.

Hell, it's dangerous. More so for him than me. But that doesn't seem to be bothering him.

He's told me time and time again that the night we met wasn't a setup like my brother and his mates think. And I hate to say it, but I believe him.

Why would he risk his life by still talking to me if there was anything adrift?

He's from a rival family. One who's making moves to take over some business on our territory from what I can figure out.

Surely, he has to actually like me to keep in contact, right?

Right?

I don't have a chance to wait for his reply. I know he's at his own party tonight and busy with his mates, so I close the app and shove my phone back in my bag, force my smile off my face and I finish up.

I pause halfway to the basins.

Was that him?

Is he Batman?

"You okay?" Emmie asks, noticing that I've paused.

"Y-yeah, sorry."

She studies me with concern but doesn't question me.

"Drinks and dancing. Let's go. And we need to find Stella."

The second we step out of the bathroom, I see him again, loitering at the end of the long hallway, watching me.

Emmie must miss him in the darkness this time because instead of pointing him out, or even leading me toward him, she drags me in the direction of the bar for alcohol, something I really can't argue with.

After three more fake blood shots, we find Stella and drag her and Seb to the dance floor.

The second we come to a stop, he drags her into his body, places his hands possessively on her hips, and dips his head to her neck.

An unhealthy wave of jealousy washes through me as I watch them.

Not because I want Seb, because I really, really don't. Him, Nico, all of them are disgusting pigs that I don't want to be anywhere near most days. The way they go through women like they're disposable is... ugh... I shiver in revulsion as the horrific image of Nico getting head from some random girl at his birthday party a few weeks ago comes back to me.

Dogs, all of them.

But despite that, what Seb and Stella seem to have found—despite all the odds against them—is exactly what I want to experience.

I don't want to go around kissing all the frogs that Knight's Ridge, hell even London, has to offer. I just want to find my prince, my knight. The one who'll put me above all the rest, who won't keep me in the shadows like everyone else in my life seems to do; but who will drag me into the light with him, and encourage me to be the person I know I can be without the overbearing weight of my family pressing down on my shoulders.

"Hey, look," Emmie says, nodding to the other side of the room.

I already know what I'm going to find when I follow her gaze. My skin is tingling with the awareness of being watched. But that doesn't mean my breath doesn't catch when I find him once again in the shadows.

He tips a black cup to his lips, downing the contents, although his eyes never leave mine. That is until mine drops when he swipes his tongue over his full bottom lip collecting up drops of whatever he just drank.

"On second thought, who gives a fuck if he's Italian, he's hot."

"You can only see his mouth, Em," I argue, although I'm not sure why.

She's right.

Every single part of me—especially the place between my thighs—knows that he's hot, just from his jawline and mouth alone.

I narrow my eyes, wishing the light was brighter so that I could see him clearly.

Is it him?

Is it Ant?

"Looks like he needs a push in the right direction," Emmie announces, dragging me toward her, throwing her arms over my shoulders and moving her body against mine.

"Whoa, how much have you had to drink?" I ask

"Not enough to think you're some hot dude who will throw me over his shoulder and have his wicked way with me," she confesses a little too seriously.

"Fair enough," I say, rolling my hips against

hers, loving the shiver that races down my spine knowing that his eyes are drilling into me.

It's an addictive feeling.

"What about you?" I shout in Emmie's ear. "Anyone catch your eye."

"Meh. We're surrounded by Knight's Ridge biggest bellends. Even the costumes can't cover their elite, conceited arses."

"Wow, you really do have a high opinion of the guys we go to school with."

"I don't want a future fucking banker, Cal. I want a man."

"Like your bad boy uncle?"

"Ew, Cal. Seriously?"

"Well, obviously not your uncle. One of his prospects."

"Prospects? You need to stop watching SoA."

I shrug. "Umm... have you seen Jax? I'm not going to be stopping anytime soon."

"So I'm not the only one who wants a bit of rough then?"

My cheeks burn red hot at her question.

"Uh... What about him?" I ask, nodding over her shoulder to a guy in a werewolf costume. Surely there's not a future banker in there."

"He's got a fucking bracelet on, Cal."

My eyes drop to where he'd shoved his costume up his arm a little to see that she's right.

"I'm going to find you a guy," I tell her.

"How about you just focus on your mystery one, and I'll sort myself out."

"Fine. Deal."

The song changes, the beat picking up and we both lose ourselves to it.

We dance until our skin is covered in sweat and my need for a new drink almost becomes unbearable.

Thankfully, right as I'm about to excuse myself to find one, a zombie appears before me and hands me a glass of blood.

"Thank you," I call, totally out of breath.

He nods and then passes another to Emmie before Stella snatches the last one from his tray seeing as she's stuck dancing with us now that her boy's been summoned by my cousin.

"How freaking awesome is this party?" I shout at my girls, the alcohol in my system more than doing its job.

"Yeah, you were right. This is pretty sweet," Stella says, glancing around before grabbing both mine and Emmie's hands and pulling us in so the three of us can dance together.

Throwing my head back, I close my eyes and just let go.

Shedding my sheltered princess skin and just enjoying being one of the girls, being out drinking when I'm underage, and partying until I can't feel my feet.

When I finally open my eyes again, I quickly discover that I'm alone.

"What the—"

I look around, not seeing anyone I recognise.

"Shit," I hiss, realising that I was probably partying a little too hard not to notice them slip away.

A flash of pink catches my eye by the door, and Emmie just shoots me a calculating smile before I sense someone step up behind me.

My entire body jolts when a large pair of burning hot hands land on my hips.

Something brushes my ear and when I spin

to see what it is, I come face to face with Batman.

His eyes lock on mine as the air crackles between us.

"You," I breathe, something settling inside me as we continue to stare at each other.

"I can't take my eyes off you, beautiful."

All the air rushes out of my lungs at his confession.

His voice, although muffled by the music, is so deep it makes the hairs on the back of my neck stand on end.

There's a flicker of familiarity within me but I push it down as he steps in front of me and drapes my arms over his shoulders so we can dance.

Wrapping his arms around my waist, he closes the space between us, pressing my body right up against his.

Our hips move together in time with the music as his dark eyes stare into mine.

My heart pounds, my pulse thundering through my veins and threatening to burn me from the inside out.

Whatever that cherry drink is ensures my

head spins and everything aside from the two of us vanishes into nothing.

One of his arms releases me before his hand cups my face.

The move is so gentle, so tender that I melt into him as his thumb brushes across my bottom lip, his eyes locked on it.

I swear to God that I actually stop breathing while a voice in my head screams for me to demand that he kisses me.

But I can't. I'm frozen in place, allowing him to take his fill.

When he finally does speak, the words that fall from his lips aren't ones that I'm expecting.

"Tell me to stop, beautiful."

"U-uh... n-no. I-I don't want you to."

All the air rushes from him, tickling across my face as he continues to study me.

"Fuck it," he breathes so quietly I almost wonder if I imagine it.

His lips brush against mine in the softest kiss and the entire world freezes around me.

We're no longer in a derelict building surrounded by people, but just the two of us alone, the rest of the world forgotten while our lips are connected.

He stills and for a split second, I think he's going to pull back having realised that he's made a mistake.

If he has any idea who I really am, then he has to know that kissing me like this is a risk. If Nico or Theo, hell any of the guys catch him, then he's possibly risking his life right now.

Reaching out, I twist the fabric of his shirt in my fingers and drag him closer, forcing him to move.

Oh fuck.

My entire body sags as his tongue brushes across my bottom lip before plunging into my mouth the second my chin drops to allow him entry.

I'll be the first to admit that I'm on the very inexperienced end of the scale when it comes to kissing, sex, anything to do with boys. But hell, this guy can kiss.

His lips move against mine as if he's speaking directly to my soul, his tongue caressing mine, kissing me with a ferocity that makes me wonder if he'd die without it.

His hand that's still at my back, drops to my arse, pinning our hips together and allowing me to feel exactly what I'm doing to him when his hard length presses against my belly.

Excitement and nerves make my stomach twist, but the heat and the ache that seem to explode in my lower belly at knowing I'm turning him on sure helps to banish any anxiety I might have about this.

A groan of frustration rumbles up my throat when he drags his lips from mine and kisses and nips across my jaw until he's at my ear.

"I need you alone," he whispers.

"Y-yes," I breathe, probably sounding like a wanton whore, but right in this moment, with his hands on me, I just don't care.

"Come on." He takes my hand and leads me toward the hallway.

I glance around, reality crashing into me for a moment and expecting every person in the room to be focused on us, but when I find them all too busy enjoying themselves, I realise that that earth-shattering kiss only tilted my world, not everyone else's.

Sensing that I've slowed, he turns back to me.

"You okay?" he asks, although I can't hear him over the music.

A smile curls at my lips as I stare at him, seeing past the mask and right into his dark eyes.

Eyes that seem to see deeper than anyone I've ever met before.

"Lead the way."

He doesn't waste any time and turns back around.

He pulls back a rope, stopping the people partying from entering before we climb a set of stairs. He pushes a door open and I stumble inside, my legs a little too unsteady in my heels after all the alcohol.

The door slams closed behind us and I only get a second to look around to see that we're in a room.

Alone.

CHAPTER THREE

"At last," he murmurs, his voice louder now that we've left the music behind.

Goose bumps erupt across my skin as he takes a step toward me.

There are no lights on up here, he's only illuminated by the silver moonlight flooding in. It makes him look dark and dangerous as he closes the space between us, his eyes roaming over my body as if I'm standing here naked for him.

Instinct makes me take a step back and a teasing smile twitches at my lips when a growl rumbles in the back of his throat.

My back bumps against the wall and I gasp

in shock.

"Just me and you now, beautiful." His voice is barely more than a growl as he rubs his thumb across his bottom lip, the move sending a bolt of desire straight to my core.

His muscular forearm ripples in the moonlight before my eyes find his once more, when he cages me in with his arms against the wall on either side of my head.

He ducks down, his lips brushing my ear.

His breath rushes across my skin, driving me freaking crazy with my need to feel his lips against mine once more.

I wait, sensing that he wants to say something.

His hand lands on my waist, his fingers dipping under the fabric of my crop top just slightly, teasing me with what might be to come.

"I'm sorry, beautiful," he finally whispers.

"Wh—" My question of why he's apologising to me is cut off when his lips find mine once more, and I damn near forget he even spoke as his tongue dives into my mouth searching mine out.

His hands slide down my body, gripping

the backs of my thighs and lifting me up the wall until they wrap around his waist, lining us up in the most incredible way.

"Oh God," I moan into his kiss as he rolls his hips, his hard length right against my core.

He kisses me like he'd literally die without it. Like I'm his air, his life raft, his fucking life support, and I am all here for it as my fingers grip his shoulders, my nails digging into the fabric of his cape, wishing it was his skin.

Finding the popper holding the fabric around his neck, I pull it open, letting it cascade to the floor.

"Fuck," he groans as I slip my hands under his shirt, his abs bunching as I push higher, already addicted to the hardness of his muscles.

Turning the tables on me, he shoves my jacket from my shoulders, his lips dropping to my neck and down my chest as I pull the garment from my wrists and throw it to the floor to join his cape.

"Oh God," I whimper when his fingers tuck under my crop top knowing that I don't have anything beneath it.

In seconds he's pulling it up my body giving me no choice but to lift my arms.

"Jesus, beautiful," he grunts, his eyes locked on mine for a beat before they drop to my bare chest. "Never needed anything so much in my entire life."

Lifting me higher as if I weigh nothing more than a feather, he kisses down my chest, over the swell of my breast before sucking one of my nipples into his mouth.

"Oh holy fuck," I gasp, my head falling back against the wall as the sensation of his hot mouth on my sensitive skin consumes my entire body.

My hand lifts without instruction from my brain, my need to thread my fingers through his hair and hold him against me to force him to continue is too much to bear, only when I connect with his mask, his hot fingers wrap around my wrist stopping me from exposing his face.

"I'll give you anything, beautiful. But not that."

His lips find mine once more as the cool night air surrounds my tender peak seconds before it brushes against his shirt making me moan once more.

He kisses me until I'm breathless again

before confessing something that makes my head spin and my limbs turn to jelly.

"I need to taste you, beautiful."

I should say no, I should demand to know who he is before letting this continue any further, but the fear of him walking away and leaving me here cold is too strong.

"Shit," I breathe, nerves hitting me like a truck. "I... uh... I've never..."

"I know," he says, hinting at the fact he is more than aware of who I am, or more so, what I do or don't do. "Let me be your first."

He gathers up my full skirt, his fingers brushing my inner thigh and going higher until he hits the soaked lace that's covering me.

"So wet for me, beautiful. I bet you taste so fucking sweet."

"Oh my God," I gasp when he rubs at me over the fabric.

"That feel good?" he whispers in my ear, the tip of his tongue tracing around the edge, making me shiver.

"Y-yes."

"Want more?"

"Oh God."

His fingers push inside my underwear,

parting my skin and finding that exact spot once more. Only, it's about a million times more intense without a barrier between us.

"Holy fuck. Fuck."

"You're even more beautiful when you're falling apart for me," he murmurs, pulling back so he can watch me.

I want to be embarrassed. I want to tell him to stop, but as something builds inside me, the promise of an epic explosion of pleasure right on the horizon, I can't find it in myself to do either of those things.

"Please," I beg. "Please, I need—"

"Shush, I've got you beautiful. Trust me." He pushes lower, spearing a finger inside me as his thumb continues circling my clit. "Let go. Let me watch you come for me."

I nod, it's the only thing I have the ability to do as his fingers rub deliciously inside of me.

I'm no stranger to what my body is capable of. I've... experimented with myself. But fuck, nothing I've done comes anywhere close to how this feels. How *he* feels.

"Oh my God."

"Come for me, beautiful."

He curls his fingers, his thumb pressing

against me harder and something inside of me shatters.

Lights flash behind my eyes as I swear something akin to fireworks erupts beneath my skin.

"Fuck, yeah. Fuck, beautiful." My hips roll, riding out the last sparks of pleasure. "Ride my hand."

He doesn't stop until my body has stopped convulsing and my orgasm has subsided.

Aftershocks race around my body as he pulls out of me, his eyes locked on mine as he lifts his fingers to his mouth.

"Oh God," I breathe as his lids lower when he sucks on them.

My lips part in shock as I stare at him unashamedly tasting me.

"More," he groans, releasing his fingers. "I need more."

"Argh," I squeal when my feet leave the floor.

He spins me around before lowering my arse onto something. A table? A dresser? I've no freaking clue but as his hand cups the back of my head and he encourages me to lie back as his mouth claims mine once again.

I can taste myself on his lips, but instead of turning me off like I thought it might, it only spurs me on.

My fingers scrabble to grab at fabric desperate to get his shirt off him, to feel his skin against mine, but any time I pull it over up his stomach he stops me from lifting it any higher.

"Please, I need—" His eyes flash with dark intent, cutting off my words as he bundles my skirt up around my waist. "Oh shit."

My knickers seem to just melt off me and the next thing I know, I'm fully exposed to him with my thighs spread wide with his giant hands.

I squirm on... whatever I'm on top of as he stares at me.

Just when I think he's not going to do anything, he murmurs, "Beautiful," before blowing a stream of hot air across my swollen pussy.

"Oh God, please."

"Only because you asked so nicely," he says, hunger and humour mixing in his deep voice.

A loud scream echoes around the empty room as his mouth connects with my core.

Oh holy fuck.

No wonder women have such good things to say about this.

His tongue laps at me like he's starving. Licking at me with the most dizzying pressure.

"You taste like heaven, beautiful."

"More," I cry, shamelessly chasing another release that's beginning to grow within me.

"You can have everything," he promises before his finger circles my entrance, pushing just inside, teasing me in the most delicious way.

Biting down on the inside of my cheek, I silently demand for him to push inside me, to find that spot he did earlier that makes my knees shake.

I wish I could call out his name, anything.

Reaching for him, my hand hits the hard plastic of his mask that is digging into my thighs but just like last time, he catches my hand before I'm able to rip it from his head.

"Why?" I cry, getting frustrated that he won't just show me his face.

What's he scared of? That I'll change my mind?

Right now, it's highly unlikely.

"Trust me," he growls, barely leaving my pussy for a second.

He ups his effort, suddenly plunging his fingers deep inside me and making my back arch off the hard surface he laid me on.

"Come for me, beautiful."

He sucks on my clit, it's almost too much, too painful but then he curls his fingers in this way that just makes me fly.

I thought my first release was intense, but it had nothing on this one as his tongue continues to flick my clit and his fingers rub my G-spot like he has a map to the freaking thing.

My entire body is covered in a sheen of sweat as I lie there with my chest heaving, desperately trying to catch my breath.

"Wow," I finally breathe when the pleasure fully subsides and he moves away from me.

He stands between my still parted legs—any shame I might have had fully gone after having his face down there while he did that—with his chin glistening in the moonlight from my wetness.

"Fuck," he barks, staring down at me, his jaw working in frustration as his fists curl at his sides.

"W-what? Did I do something wrong?" I ask, my cheeks heating. I'm thankful that it's dark enough that he can't actually see.

A small laugh falls from his lips as he rubs at the back of his neck almost nervously.

"No, beautiful. You're perfect. Too fucking perfect."

Sensing him shutting down, I rush to sit up.

"What's wrong?" I ask, my heart damn near jumping into my throat when his eyes flick to the door. "N-no, don't leave. P-please."

"I shouldn't have even brought you up here. I shouldn't be here with you."

"Why? Who are you?"

"No one who you should let touch you, let alone beg to stay."

"Says who?"

"Me."

He takes a step back and the icy claws of fear begin to take hold, threatening to freeze my almost boiling blood in an instant.

"I want you to be my first," I blurt out. It might be a rash decision, but I know it's right. I know it's what I want. "Please."

"You've no idea what you're asking for."

"No? Maybe not. But how about you show me. I want you."

"Fuck."

He spins away from me and stops in front of the window, his fingers curling around the frame, the muscles in his shoulders pulled tight.

"I-I don't care who you are. I want this. Please."

Slowly, he looks over his shoulder. His square jaw set as if he's already made his decision and when his eyes meet mine, a shiver of need races down my spine.

"I want you," I repeat. "Give me everything."

He's on me before I even have a chance to blink. His lips devouring mine once more as I reach for his waistband.

It takes my useless fingers longer than it should to open the button and drag the zip of his fly down but I get the most incredible reward when I finally do and push my hand inside his underwear because the moan that rips up his throat is something I'm never going to forget.

My fingers wrap around his thick length,

and I gasp, feeling the sheer size of him.

My stomach clenches with nerves, but I know that I'm not going to go back on this now.

What I told him was true. I want this.

Him.

Us.

Even if it is just for tonight. Even if I never find out who he is.

No matter what happens next, I know I'll always treasure this night. The night I pushed aside all my insecurities, my fears, my timid existence and became the woman I've always wanted to be.

I've no idea what I'm doing, I just let my instincts take over as I stroke down the length of his cock while he awkwardly shoves his jeans over his hips, freeing his length while his other hand is twisted in my hair, holding me exactly where he wants me.

"I-I don't have any condoms," he confesses into our kiss.

"I'm on the pill. And I'm a virgin so I'm pretty sure I'm clean."

"Fuck, beautiful. I shouldn't be doing this. You're too good for me."

"Are you clean?" I ask, my voice a little

more forceful than he was expecting.

He pulls back from our kiss and stares down into my eyes.

"Yes, but—"

"I trust you."

"Biggest mistake of your life, beautiful."

But in contrast to his words, his thumb brushes over my cheek and then my swollen bottom lip as if I'm the most precious thing in the world.

"You're going to regret this," he tells me, his voice full of self-loathing.

Mimicking his move, I cup his face. "Never. You're giving me more than you could ever know."

His eyes hold mine for a second longer before he makes his decision.

Moving his hands to my arse, he drags me right to the edge of the surface, and steps into my body.

"Lie back," he instructs.

Releasing him, I do as I'm told, resting back on my elbows so I can watch.

He stares down at where we're about to be connected almost as if he's in a trance as he rubs the head of his cock through my wetness.

"You deserve more than this, Calli."

I gasp at the use of my name.

It proves one thing.

He knows exactly who I am, and just what might happen to him if the guys find out about this.

But despite his words, he lowers his length to my entrance. His eyes locked on mine, his jaw flexing with the restraint I'm sure it's taking him not to just thrust straight inside me.

"Please," I whimper, my muscles rippling, desperate to know how he's going to feel inside me. "I want you. I want you inside me."

"Jesus, fuck. Fuck," he barks out but he doesn't step away like I fear, instead he pushes inside me, but only a little and nowhere near enough.

"Please," I beg, digging my heels into his arse to make him move.

But just before I think he's going to surge forward, loud footsteps race across the bare floorboard outside the door.

"Someone's shooting. Let's go."

His eyes go wide, his entire body tensing with those four words.

It's almost like a bucket of water has just

been thrown over both of us.

"Fuck. I'm sorry. I'm so sorry."

In a flash, he's got his jeans back on and he's racing toward the door.

A little light from out in the hallway shines through the room, but it's still not enough to be able to identify him, and then he's gone, the door slamming behind him.

Male voices continue shouting as the footsteps begin to fade away as they race down the stairs.

"FUCK," I scream, covering my face with my hands.

Guilt swamps me because I just told him that I wouldn't regret this, and yet that's exactly what I'm fucking doing. Although not because we did it, but because we never got the chance to finish it.

A thought hits me and I jump up from whatever I'm on and race toward the window, my legs damn near giving out as I wobble on my heels.

My breath catches when I see men racing toward the treeline and disappearing into the darkness all with their guns raised in front of them.

My heart sinks into my stomach knowing that my brother, my cousin, and the others are probably going to be in the middle of all of that.

My blood runs cold with the thought that they could get hurt.

Or worse.

I might make out like I hate them, but the reality is, they're my family. And I couldn't imagine my life without the arseholes in it.

But then, I see *him* race across the garden. I've no idea how I know it's him. It's so dark that they're all just figures cutting through the night, but I know.

He does too.

Because right before he disappears into the treeline, he looks back, and right at me.

All my breath comes out in a rush as our eyes collide.

Holy shit.

Calli and her mystery Knight's story will continues in

DARK KNIGHT

ABOUT THE AUTHOR

Tracy Lorraine is a *USA Today* and *Wall Street Journal* bestselling new adult and contemporary romance author. Tracy has recently turned thirty and lives in a cute Cotswold village in England with her husband, baby girl and lovable but slightly crazy dog. Having always been a bookaholic with her head stuck in her Kindle, Tracy decided to try her hand at a story idea she dreamt up and hasn't looked back since.

Be the first to find out about new releases and offers. Sign up to my newsletter here.

If you want to know what I'm up to and see teasers and snippets of what I'm working on, then you need to be in my Facebook group. Join Tracy's Angels here.

Keep up to date with Tracy's books at

www.tracylorraine.com

ALSO BY TRACY LORRAINE

Falling Series

Falling for Ryan: Part One #1

Falling for Ryan: Part Two #2

Falling for Jax #3

Falling for Daniel (A Falling Series Novella)

Falling for Ruben #4

Falling for Fin #5

Falling for Lucas #6

Falling for Caleb #7

Falling for Declan #8

Falling For Liam #9

Forbidden Series

Falling for the Forbidden #1

Losing the Forbidden #2

Fighting for the Forbidden #3

Craving Redemption #4

Demanding Redemption #5

Avoiding Temptation #6

Chasing Temptation #7

Rebel Ink Series

Hate You #1

Trick You #2

Defy You #3

Play You #4

Inked (A Rebel Ink/Driven Crossover)

Rosewood High Series

Thorn #1

Paine #2

Savage #3

Fierce #4

Hunter #5

Faze (#6 Prequel)

Fury #6

Legend #7

Maddison Kings University Series

TMYM: Prequel

TRYS #1

TDYW #2

TBYS #3

TVYC #4

TDYD #5

TDYR #6

TRYD #7

Knight's Ridge Empire Series

Wicked Summer Knight: Prequel (Stella & Seb)

Wicked Knight #1 (Stella & Seb)

Wicked Princess #2 (Stella & Seb)

Wicked Empire #3 (Stella & Seb)

Deviant Knight #4 (Emmie & Theo)

Deviant Princess #5 (Emmie & Theo

Deviant Reign #6 (Emmie & Theo)

One Reckless Knight (Jodie & Toby)

Reckless Knight #7 (Jodie & Toby)

Reckless Princess #8 (Jodie & Toby)

Reckless Dynasty #9 (Jodie & Toby)

Dark Knight #10 (Calli & Batman)

Ruined Series

Ruined Plans #1

Ruined by Lies #2

Ruined Promises #3

Never Forget Series

Never Forget Him #1

Never Forget Us #2

Everywhere & Nowhere #3

Chasing Series

Chasing Logan

The Cocktail Girls

His Manhattan

Her Kensington

THORN

SNEAK PEEK

CHAPTER ONE

Amalie

"I think you'll really enjoy your time here," Principal Hartmann says. He tries to sound cheerful about it, but he's got sympathy oozing from his wrinkled, tired eyes.

This shouldn't have been part of my life. I should be in London starting university, yet here I am at the beginning of what is apparently my junior year at an American high school I have no idea about aside from its name and the fact my mum attended many years ago. A lump climbs up my throat as thoughts of my parents hit me without warning.

"I know things are going to be different and you might feel that you're going backward, but I can assure you it's the right thing to do. It will give you the time you need to… adjust and to put some serious thought into what you want to do once you graduate."

Time to adjust. I'm not sure any amount of time will be enough to learn to live without my parents and being shipped across the Pacific to start a new life in America.

"I'm sure it'll be great." Plastering a fake smile on my face, I take the timetable from the principal's hand and stare down at it. The butterflies that were already fluttering around in my stomach erupt to the point I might just throw up over his chipped Formica desk.

Math, English lit, biology, gym, my hands tremble until I see something that instantly relaxes me, *art and film studies.* At least I got my own way with something.

"I've arranged for someone to show you around. Chelsea is the captain of the cheer squad, what she doesn't know about the school isn't worth knowing. If you need anything, Amalie, my door is always open."

Nodding at him, I rise from my chair just as a soft knock sounds out and a cheery brunette bounces into the room. My knowledge of American high schools comes courtesy of the hours of films I used to spend my evenings watching, and she fits the stereotype of captain to a tee.

"You wanted something, Mr. Hartmann?" she sings so sweetly it makes even my teeth shiver.

"Chelsea, this is Amalie. It's her first day starting junior year. I trust you'll be able to show her around. Here's a copy of her schedule."

"Consider it done, sir."

"I assured Amalie that she's in safe hands."

I want to say it's my imagination but when she turns her big chocolate eyes on me, the light in them diminishes a little.

"Lead the way." My voice is lacking any kind of enthusiasm and from the narrowing of her eyes, I don't think she misses it.

I follow her out of the room with a little less

bounce in my step. Once we're in the hallway, she turns her eyes on me. She's really quite pretty with thick brown hair, large eyes, and full lips. She's shorter than me, but then at five foot eight, you'll be hard pushed to find many other teenage girls who can look me in the eye.

Tilting her head so she can look at me, I fight my smile. "Let's make this quick. It's my first day of senior year and I've got shit to be doing."

Spinning on her heels, she takes off and I rush to catch up with her. "Cafeteria, library." She points then looks down at her copy of my timetable. "Looks like your locker is down there." She waves her hand down a hallway full of students who are all staring our way, before gesturing in the general direction of my different subjects.

"Okay, that should do it. Have a great day." Her smile is faker than mine's been all morning, which really is saying something. She goes to walk away, but at the last minute turns back to me. "Oh, I forgot. That over there." I follow her finger as she points to a large group of people outside the open double doors sitting around a bunch of tables. "That's *my* group. I should probably warn you now that you won't fit in there."

I hear her warning loud and clear, but it didn't really need saying. I've no intention of befriending the cheerleaders, that kind of thing's not really my scene. I'm much happier hiding behind my camera and slinking into the background.

Chelsea flounces off and I can't help my eyes from following her out toward *her* group. I can see from here that it consists of her squad and the football team. I can also see the longing in other student's eyes as they walk past them. They either want to be them or want to be part of their stupid little gang.

Jesus, this place is even more stereotypical than I was expecting.

Unfortunately, my first class of the day is in the direction Chelsea just went. I pull my bag up higher on my shoulder and hold the couple of books I have tighter to my chest as I walk out of the doors.

I've not taken two steps out of the building when my skin tingles with awareness. I tell myself to keep my head down. I've no interest in being their entertainment but my eyes defy me, and I find myself looking up as Chelsea points at me and laughs. I knew my sudden arrival in the town wasn't a secret. My mum's legacy is still strong, so when they heard the news, I'm sure it was hot gossip.

Heat spreads from my cheeks and down my neck. I go to look away when a pair of blue eyes catch my attention. While everyone else's look intrigued, like they've got a new pet to play with, his are haunted and angry. Our stare holds, his eyes narrow as if he's trying to warn me of something before he menacingly shakes his head.

Confused by his actions, I manage to rip my eyes from his and turn toward where I think I should be going.

I only manage three steps at the most before I crash into something—or somebody.

"Shit, I'm sorry. Are you okay?" a deep voice asks. When I look into the kind green eyes of the guy in front of me, I almost sigh with relief. I was starting to wonder if I'd find anyone who wasn't just going to glare at me. I know I'm the new girl but shit. They must experience new kids on a weekly basis, I can't be that unusual.

"I'm fine, thank you."

"You're the new British girl. Emily, right?"

"It's Amalie, and yeah... that's me."

"I'm so sorry about your parents. Mom said she was friends with yours." Tears burn my eyes. Today is hard enough without the constant reminder of everything I've lost. "Shit, I'm sorry. I shouldn't have—"

"It's fine," I lie.

"What's your first class?"

Handing over my timetable, he quickly runs his eyes over it. "English lit, I'm heading that way. Can I walk you?"

"Yes." His smile grows at my eagerness and for the first time today my returning one is almost sincere.

"I'm Shane, by the way." I look over and smile at him, thankfully the hallway is too noisy for us to continue any kind of conversation.

He seems like a sweet guy but my head's spinning and just the thought of trying to hold a serious conversation right now is exhausting.

Student's stares follow my every move. My skin prickles as more and more notice me as I walk beside Shane. Some give me smiles but most just nod in my direction, pointing me out to their friends. Some are just downright rude and physically point at me like I'm some fucking zoo animal awoken from its slumber.

In reality, I'm just an eighteen-year-old girl who's starting somewhere new, and desperate to blend into the crowd. I know that with who I am—or more who my parents were—that it's not going to be all that easy, but I'd at least like a chance to try to be normal. Although I fear I might have lost that the day I lost my parents.

"This is you." Shane's voice breaks through my thoughts and when I drag my head up from avoiding everyone else around me, I see he's holding the door open.

Thankfully the classroom's only half full, but still, every single set of eyes turn to me.

Ignoring their attention, I keep my head down and find an empty desk toward the back of the room.

Once I'm settled, I risk looking up. My breath catches when I find Shane still standing in the doorway, forcing the students entering to squeeze past him. He nods his head. I know it's his way of asking if I'm okay. Forcing a smile onto my lips, I nod in return and after a few seconds, he turns to leave.

THORN and the rest of the ROSEWOOD series are now LIVE.

DOWNLOAD TO CONTINUE READING

Printed in Dunstable, United Kingdom

76956466R00048